A KING'S RANSOM

An IN THE CARDS Story

OTHER BOOKS BY
JEFF VANOUDENHOVE

SERIES

THE DARK SERIES

Dark Place
Dark Lane
Dark Queen
Dark Child
The Final Dark

THE ALPHABET KILLER SERIES

The Alphabet Killer
The Letter Man
Killer by Number

STANDALONE NOVELS

Just Listen

Emma

Reaper House

The Disappearing

SHORT STORY COLLECTION

Screams in the Dark and Other Twisted Tales

COLLABORATIONS

Horror for the Holidays

COMING SOON

Zero Tolerance

A KING'S RANSOM

An IN THE CARDS Story

Jeff VanOudenhove

Westfield, MA

JAVO Publication
Westfield, Massachusetts 01085

This is a work of fiction. The characters, places, and events portrayed in this book are either the product of the author's imagination or are used fictitiously. Any similarity to real persons, living or dead, business establishments, or events is coincidental and not intended by the author.

ISBN: 979-8-9918888-9-9

Cover design by M.A. Green

*For all those who carry a heavier burden
than others will ever know*

Chapter 1

Westley looked to his left shoulder, where the battle-worn fingers dug into his skin through his neatly-ironed dress shirt, a subtle reminder of who was in charge. He winced.

"Is everything all right?" Gabby asked from across the table after noticing his awkward reaction.

Westley immediately snapped his attention forward, peering at his blind date over the lit candle sprouting from the flowery centerpiece.

"Oh, ah, yeah," he replied sheepishly, ignoring the pain and the stern hand that dealt it. "So, I was thinking, perhaps after dinner, we could go for a stroll along the boardwalk."

"I'd love that," Gabby replied, reaching for her glass of Chardonnay. "It's such a beautiful night."

"Yes, it is." Westley felt himself swallow as he nervously pulled at the front of his shirt collar to loosen the grip his tie had around his neck. He tilted his chin upward and slightly to the left, tucking his eyebrows. "Are you sure?" he murmured under his breath.

Gabby lowered her drink beside the salad plate, offering an inquisitive glare.

"What was that?" she asked.

Westley snatched the cloth napkin from his lap and quickly wiped his lips while clearing his throat.

"Oh, um, I was just asking if you were sure you didn't want another glass of wine."

Gabby's eyes drifted to her still-half-full glass. She pursed her lips and raised her left eyebrow questioningly.

"Um...no," she doled out slowly, giving Westley a sympathetic glance as if to let him know she understood his nervousness. "I think this one will be enough."

"Oh, right," Westley responded with an uneasy chuckle. "Forgive me. Can you tell it's been a while since I've been on a real date?" He suddenly dipped his left shoulder and scrunched his face as if he were in pain, then excitedly added in a raised voice, "I mean, with someone so beautiful!"

Gabby flinched, taken aback by Westley's pronounced outburst. Slowly, a smile crept onto her face.

"Th-thank you," she stuttered, half-shocked, half-flattered. "Are you sure you're all right?" Gabby questioned, a concerned look in her eyes. She gestured with her index finger toward his left shoulder.

Westley's eyes grew wide as he swiveled his head sideways to where she had pointed, afraid she knew more than what she let on.

"You seem like you're in pain," Gabby continued.

Relief washed over him, as did the sweat quickly seeping from his pores, soaking into the fibers of his undershirt.

"Oh, that," he returned with a discomfited grin. "It's an old injury. Comes and goes."

"If it's bothering you, we don't have to go for that walk."

"No!" he blurted. Then, in a quieter tone, added, "I mean, no, it's fine. It'll be fine. The walk will take my mind off of it and help ease the pain. But, if you'll excuse me, I have to use the restroom."

His lovely date nodded. "Sure."

Westley rose from his chair and placed the linen napkin on his empty bread plate. He pressed his lips together while gauging his date's reaction. He needed a respite. The last thing he wanted was to scare her away. That wouldn't work in his favor. The consequences were too high. The bothersome distraction he'd been enduring, however, was a little much and needed to be handled delicately before further damage resulted in an outcome that was less than satisfactory. He faked a smile as he often did, and strolled toward the men's room.

Feeling the weight of his follower close behind, Westley pushed the door open and immediately bent over, checking for legs under each of the stalls. When he determined the bathroom was free of unwanted patrons, he let out a heavy breath and faced the large mirror over the three-sink vanity. His eyes narrowed and focused on the reflection, peering over his shoulder at the menacing sight behind him. Westley may have been the only person present in the men's room, but he definitely wasn't alone.

Chapter 2

The air grew thin in the confined walls of the restroom. A chill swept over Westley as he stared intently at the grand orchestrator of the evening. The large presence of an aged man stood firm, looming over his shoulder threateningly, gripping the handle of a silver longsword sheathed on his hip. The sizeable being, masked behind a thick ivory mustache and beard, was draped in a velvety green cape accentuated with gold stitching along the hem of the fabric. The adornment lay over his shoulders, partially obstructing a tarnished armor plate strapped across his chest. On his head, a lusterless crown of gold, faded and weathered with time. The figure expanded his torso outward to assert authority as he sneered disapprovingly at Westley's reflection.

"You don't understand," Westley griped in a hushed voice. "Things are different now. You have to be patient in these situations."

A guttural snarl erupted from the large man while his eyes flashed with a burning, white glow. He spoke not a word, yet Westley could hear every forceful command through the silence.

"I *will*," Westley snipped through gritted teeth. "I told you I would do it. Haven't I already proven myself? Things like this take time."

The bearded figure's lips moved as if he were speaking, but with no sound.

"I can't do that," Westley responded. "A lot has changed since back in your day. People can't just take whoever they want and drag them back to their stone castle. Nowadays, it requires a bit more finesse."

The older man's eyes crackled and sparked with arcane energy as he curled his upper lip.

"No!" Westley shouted. "I won't let you do that. Let me handle it."

The noticeably angry figure's hand clenched tighter around the longsword's hilt, his fingers turning pale from squeezing the blood from them. Westley's eyes darted to the weapon just as the large, ominous being yanked it free from its leather-bound wooden scabbard.

"Stop!" Westley yelled, his eyes full and round. "You wanted me to do this; I'm doing it. But it's gotta be my way." His words echoed off the tile walls of the empty bathroom. Another restaurant patron entered just as Westley's next words escaped from his lips. "Put your sword back in your pants."

The man who entered froze, staring side-eyed at Westley while crinkling his brow. Westley felt his cheeks burn red with embarrassment.

"Oh, sorry. Not you," Westley assured the man, who glanced around the empty room. "I mean, not anyone else, either," Westley continued nervously. "I was practicing my lines for an upcoming audition."

The man nodded and flashed a skeptical grin as he cautiously inched past Westley on his way to the farthest urinal. Westley shifted his attention to the unseen behemoth of a man still clutching the sword, and then veered his eyes to the vacant scabbard on his hip in an attempt to encourage the threatening figure to sheath the weapon. The ancient figure huffed through clenched teeth before complying with Westley's unspoken request. Westley's shoulders dropped in relief.

"Now, can we get out of here, please?"

Westley reached for the door before waiting for an answer, but turned to the man at the far urinal and shouted, "Again, not you."

Storming from the restroom, Westley felt as though he were being prodded in the back like cattle being led to a slaughterhouse. The large presence behind him, a king among commoners, a relic of medieval times, manipulated his every step.

Summoned by some unknown force out of time and place, the royal sovereign demanded servitude from his loyal pet, or the punishment would be severe. A heavy price was cast, a ransom owed in blood. Death sought its next resident, and it was time to pay. Westley bargained for his life, but the bill was due. A body must be vanquished, snuffed out of existence. The decree was clear: to spare himself, another must take his place. Though it weighed heavily upon him, Westley knew his future actions were a necessary burden he'd have to bear.

He arrived back at the table with a cool smile on his face, flashing his dimples over the candlelight, his true motives as invisible as the phantom king guiding his misdeeds. Westley traced his index finger over the top of his date's hand before gently clasping her fingers in his palm. Leading with a flirtatious wink, Westley spoke.

"How about you and I get out of here?"

Chapter 3

Like a gentleman, Westley held the restaurant door open for Gabby as they exited into the calm night. She smiled, squeezing the front flaps of her thin, fall jacket together with one hand, while she slung her small designer purse over her shoulder with the other. There was a subtle breeze, salty and warm, careening in from the oceanside pier. The mile-long boardwalk hugged the asphalt at the edge of the sandy beach, its treated wood winding a romantic path along a small strip of Atlantic coast for both residents and tourists alike, ending at the rear of the lavish Royal Crestwood Hotel parking lot.

Westley took his place by Gabby's side, timidly tucking his hands into the pockets of his khaki pants. His shoulders tightened nervously as he struggled with his thoughts, searching for something to say to the innocent woman by his side, with whom he had immoral plans.

"It's, ah.., it sure is beautiful out this evening," he fumbled with his words, gazing out over the foam-covered waves.

"Yes," Gabby replied. "It's so calm, and even when there's a breeze, it feels unseasonably warm for this time of year."

"Have you been out this way before?" Westley asked.

"Not since I was a teenager," Gabby replied. "My friends and I drove up here the week before graduation to spend the weekend. Gosh, I guess it's been, what, fifteen years now. How about you?"

"Oh yeah," he answered with an assertive nod. "I come out here quite often to get away from the monotony of my everyday life. Package Engineering isn't exactly exciting. Sometimes I need to get out of my own head, you know? Coming here allows me to leave all that stuff behind."

"Yeah, I know what you mean."

They continued along the boardwalk, sauntering in an awkward silence, the hushed space between them broken up only by the sound of the incoming waves. Westley could feel the ominous presence lingering behind him, relaying urgent demands in his ear. His breathing became heavier as frustration mounted until he couldn't take the emperor's harsh words anymore.

"Will you stop?" he raised his voice.

Gabby froze for a moment, taking a slight step away from Westley's side. Her right hand swung up to her purse strap as if she suddenly feared it being snatched from her.

Westley caught her reaction, the unease on her face. To cover himself, he continued, but in a quieter voice.

"I mean, just for a moment to take it all in." He turned his gaze to the sky. "The stars are amazingly bright tonight."

Gabby hesitantly tilted her chin upward, her eyes shifting between the heavenly constellations and her peculiar date.

"There's something magical about them, don't you think?" Westley stated.

"Yeah," Gabby answered. "I guess I never take the time to admire what's right over my head."

"Oh, we'll have to change that," Westley said in a mild tone behind a soft but excited chuckle. Gabby watched Westley's expression as he stared skyward in childlike wonder, an inviting smile taking shape on his face. In that moment, her nerves washed away like the ocean's breeze caressing over her shoulders.

"You're a hopeless romantic, aren't you?" Gabby said with a contented smile on her face.

Westley paused his stargazing to look at the beautiful woman sharing his company. His lips formed a coy smirk as he wrinkled his nose in thought.

"I guess maybe I am, yeah," he responded. "Is that a bad thing?"

"No," Gabby quickly replied. "It's not a bad thing at all. Compared to some of the dates I've had, it's quite refreshing, actually."

Westley fell silent, dropping his chin to his chest.

"Oh, I'm sorry," Gabby continued. "I shouldn't have mentioned anything about other dates. Believe me, they weren't anyth..."

"It's not that," Westley interjected.

"Oh, then what's wrong?"

"Nothing," he replied, raising his eyes to meet hers. "It's just that.., I'm having a wonderful time with you, and I know at some point the evening will come to an end."

Gabby flashed a faux frown with a twinge of bliss underneath. Then, her face lit up in a full smile.

"Well, until then, would you like to hold my hand while we continue walking?" she asked.

"Y-yes," Westley stuttered. "I'd like that very much."

He extended his hand for hers, but she held up her index finger to stop him.

"Wait!"

She bent over to slip her heels off. While she did, Westley enjoyed the scenery, admiring her shapely legs and the way her tight skirt hugged the curve of her ass.

"I've wanted to do this all night," Gabby admitted. "These things are *killing* me."

Westley noticed how "killing" was deepened and drawn out in her voice, and he couldn't help but grin at the irony of her word choice. He looked over his shoulder at his ominous chaperone and sneered devilishly.

"There; that's better," Gabby said with relief in her voice, her toes freely wiggling within her stockings. She draped her pink shoes at her right side, the high heels dangling from her first two fingers. Then she extended her other hand and rapidly clapped her fingers against her open palm to convey an obvious message. "Now I'm ready."

Westley smiled and eased his hand into Gabby's, gently mingling his fingers with hers. She returned a similar smile as they began to walk onward into the night.

"Are you happy now?" Westley asked.

"I am," Gabby replied, not realizing Westley's question wasn't directed toward her, but to the figure following close behind, waiting for his puppet to exact a heavy price.

Chapter 4

The couple walked along the boardwalk, admiring and enjoying the ocean, the sky, and each other's company, until finally reaching the Royal Crestwood Hotel grounds. The luxury hotel offered oceanside view accommodations and easy access to the popular boardwalk just off the rear of the parking lot, New Hampshire's version of Maine's Marginal Way.

Gabby stared in awe at the magnificent building, admiring the Victorian-style architecture and the fine details in the woodwork and exterior accents.

"This place is gorgeous," Gabby said, her eyes wide and sparkling under the hotel's exterior lights.

"It is," Westley replied. "Would you like to check out the interior?"

"Don't tell me you're staying here," Gabby said.

"No," Westley answered, surprised at his date's comment. "This place is too rich for my blood," he added. "My place is only a couple of miles from here."

"Oh, you're close."

"I am."

"No wonder you're able to get out here so often."

"Still not as often as I'd like," Westley stated. "But I did park here before walking to meet you at the restaurant."

"You walked there?" Gabby questioned, flabbergasted.

"I did, but I won't lie; It's more motivating when you're in the company of a beautiful woman." He smiled and winked.

Gabby dipped her chin so he couldn't see her blushing cheeks.

"So, how about it?" Westley asked.

"How about what?"

"Would you like to go inside and check the place out?"

"Oh my God, I'd love it!"

"Let's go, then."

Westley tugged on Gabby's arm as he strode forward across the parking lot with determination, ignoring the grunts and protests of the elder liege at his heels. He knew his mission, and he wasn't going to let an impatient ruler from a bygone era rush him into ruining the only opportunity he had. Gabby was his last chance at surviving the night. Everything needed to be perfect if he was going to win her over and gain her trust.

They reached the entrance to the extravagant hotel when Gabby froze, staring nervously through the large glass doors.

"Shit!" she vocalized without realizing.

"What is it?" Westley asked.

She quickly side-stepped, ducking behind a wide, ornate pillar to the right of the entryway, and pressed her back against its cold, granite surface.

"Shit! Shit!" she repeated, peeking around the structure to get a glimpse into the lobby.

"What?" Westley questioned. "What's wrong?"

Gabby looked at him with a nervous expression on her face, her lips displaced, showing her clenched teeth.

"That guy at the check-in desk," she replied, "the one with that trampy-looking girl wearing the red dress."

Westley took another glance through the glass doors at who she was referring to.

"That's my ex-boyfriend," she continued.

"That guy with the barely-legal-looking blonde hanging off his arm?"

"Yup, that's him. And girls like that are the reason why he's my ex. He was always sniffing out the young ones, and then didn't have enough control to keep it in his pants. I only wish I knew sooner. Who knows how many easily charmed twenty-somethings he'd been with before I found out how much of a dirtbag he was?"

Westley continued to peer into the hotel, watching the couple intently, anger welling up in his chest. He couldn't help but think about how Gabby's ex might have just cost him his only hope of fending off death. He understood Gabby's resentment toward the man. He didn't even know him, and already, he wanted to kill him.

"It looks like they've finished checking in," Westley relayed. "They're heading to the elevators. We can still go inside if you'd like." He was trying to salvage whatever he could from the uncomfortable situation.

"No," Gabby responded. "I don't want to be anywhere near that man or risk running into him."

"I understand," Westley said in a sorrowful tone, as his attention shifted sideways, eyeballing the white-bearded emperor, who grabbed the handle of his longsword, once again. Swallowing hard, Westley continued. "I can walk you back to your car, or I can drive you back if you'd prefer."

Gabby stood silent for a moment, surveying Westley's sullen features. She could tell he was disappointed in how the evening shifted. In truth, she was disappointed, too. But it didn't have to end on a dour note. She reached forward and clasped onto Westley's hand, flashing him an apologetic grin.

"I'm sorry about my reaction," she offered. "You said your place was just a couple of miles from here?"

"Yeah," he responded with a nod.

"Do you have any coffee?" she asked.

He plastered a huge smile on his face while pointing his thumb at his chest. "Crazy coffee drinker here," he announced.

"Well, good," she replied, holding back a chuckle. "You can make me a cup then."

"You got it," Westley said excitedly. "Would you like to ride with me or follow in your...?"

"I can ride with you," Gabby jumped in. "If you don't mind driving me back to my car later."

"Not at all," he assured her, leading the way to his vehicle with a little pep in his step. He wasn't so much excited about the coffee as he was about his plan coming together unexpectedly. It was better than he'd hoped. He was taking his date back to his place, where they could be alone, secluded, without the worry of a second vehicle in his driveway looking conspicuous. He glanced over his shoulder at the unseen armored king, his face dripping with smug delight as he smiled.

The war-ravaged sovereign narrowed his eyes at the arrogance of his lowly dog. His pet had done well. Soon, the debt Westley owed would be washed away with the woman's blood.

Chapter 5

Westley's eyes kept shifting nervously to the rearview mirror, gleaning his royal passenger's discomfort. The large regal figure sat hunched in the back seat, his crown scraping the ceiling of the mid-sized sedan. Glowing eyes burned with discontent, causing Westley to squirm in his seat while his fingers tapped anxiously on the steering wheel. His odd behavior and uneasy, lingering stares in the mirror didn't go unnoticed by Gabby. During one of Westley's extended glares in the rearview, Gabby turned and peered over her shoulder, first into the empty backseat, and then out the rear window to the vacant street behind them.

"Is everything all right?" she asked. "You seem distracted."

"What?" Westley questioned, her words catching him off guard, percolating in his head while his brain raced for a reasonable explanation for his aloof behavior. "Oh, no, I'm…"

"If you're uncomfortable with me coming over..," she interjected.

"No!" he responded quickly, cutting her off before she could finish. "I *want* you to come over."

"But you keep looking back as if you're having second thoughts."

"No, no, not at all," he replied, digging deep for something to relieve her doubts. "I'm sorry if I seem a little out of sorts. It's my imaginary friend back there." He shot his thumb over his shoulder while displaying a cockeyed grin.

"Your what?" Gabby asked, glancing into the backseat again, showing concern.

"I'm just playing," Westley assured her. "But you know how you sometimes get that voice whispering in your ear, telling you all the right or wrong things you're doing? Mine keeps telling me not to screw this up. As I mentioned, it's been a while since I've dated. I don't want anything to ruin the evening." He squinted his eyes back at the mirror. "Not even *you* back there," he stated behind a fake chortle.

Gabby giggled, letting her worries dissipate. She recognized her date was nervous. *She* was, too. She didn't make it a habit to invite herself over to a man's house on a first date, but something was telling her this could be the one. She didn't want to let the opportunity slip away because of his eccentricities.

They arrived at a little ranch house in a quiet neighborhood. It was early enough that all his neighbors were still awake, but late enough that none of them would be outdoors. That was perfect, Westley thought. Nobody would be around to notice he'd brought home a guest. Nobody would be the wiser when that guest was never heard from again.

"Don't mind the mess," Westley stated, opening the front door for his date. "The cleaning lady only comes during a full moon. When it falls on a Tuesday. During a leap year." He tried to bury his nerves behind his wit, but the damp circles under his armpits gave him away. After Gabby had entered, she noticed how Westley had held the door open for a few seconds longer. With an amused smile, she questioned, "For your imaginary friend?"

Her comment caught Westley by surprise, who stumbled with his response.

"Oh, ha ha, um, yeah, something like that."

"That's too bad," she replied flirtatiously. "I was hoping we could be alone."

Westley's eyes grew larger. "Oh, consider him gone then."

As Gabby turned to look around Westley's quaint little house, Westley shifted his attention to the ethereal monarch and shook his head in denial of his previous remarks. Not that he had a say. The emperor of old would do *what* he wanted, *when* he wanted. His deal was with Westley, which meant Westley's actions, his very life, were forfeit, unless he could find another to take his place. The woman would be an acceptable offering. He allowed his forsaken subject some latitude to accomplish the sacrifice.

"This is a great place you have," Gabby affirmed, nodding her head as she glanced around the living space.

"Thank you," Westley replied.

It's true, he spruced up his home a bit in advance of the hopeful outcome. He wanted it to look comfortable and appealing before things became...messy.

"Please, make yourself at home." He gestured to a brown leather sofa adorned with light tan accent pillows and a neatly folded throw blanket across the rear. "Now, for the coffee, would you like regular, decaf, or full-on diesel?"

"Regular will be fine," she said with a smile. "I'll need the caffeine to stay awake. I've got a little bit of a drive for me later."

"Yes, right. Of course." Westley stepped away toward the kitchen, speaking over his shoulder as he did. "One regular coming up."

As he filled the coffee maker reservoir with water, the monarch's looming presence stood rigid by his side, observing Westley's peculiar activities, and speaking words only Westley could hear.

"I know," Westley whispered, not wanting to alert his guest in the other room. "I've gotten her this far. The rest will be easy."

He listened to his liege's commands, his heart rate increasing with each decree from the aged warrior.

"That wasn't part of the deal," Westley argued quietly, reaching into a cabinet drawer and pulling out a steak knife. "I should get it over with quickly." He made two motions with the knife to visually explain his intentions.

First, he jabbed it forward in the air as if to signify stabbing his victim. Then he brought the knife several inches in front of his neck and quickly yanked his arm sideways to suggest slicing her throat. Both were met with a low guttural rumble, rising from the depths of the bitter ruler's gullet.

In another life, another place, this king had ruled with an iron fist. His methods were cruel and sadistic. In his own time, the killing of an enemy was not a merciful act. An example had to be made, and in this new setting, in this modern time, since he couldn't do it himself, Westley would be the emperor's hand.

"All right, all right," Westley mumbled under his breath. "I'll do it."

Then, he heard his date call out from the other room. "I'm sorry, did you say something?"

Westley flashed an annoyed look at the king before replying.

"Oh, ah, I was asking if you'd like milk or sugar," Westley recovered.

The sovereign behemoth stood down, backing away from his compliant pet.

"Black is fine, thank you," Gabby responded. Westley opened another drawer to the left of the silverware and pulled out a roll of duct tape. He placed it on the counter as the coffee finished brewing. He poured two coffee cups, one black and one with a little something special, then returned the pot to its burner. He took a deep breath, placed the steak knife beside the roll of tape, then rehearsed a phony smile. He didn't want to appear more nervous than he already was. He grabbed the cups from the counter and released his breath, along with some pent-up anxiety. A piercing thought entered his mind as he exited the kitchen and spotted Gabby relaxing at the far end of the sofa, smiling intently at his return.

The fun was about to begin.

Chapter 6

Westley watched his guest sip the coffee nice and slow, the way her glossy lips caressed the rim of the cup, leaving the slightest outline of her makeup on the mug. He felt himself getting aroused as Gabby's tongue washed away the excess liquid from her lips after each sip. He had to be careful with his lustful stares. He realized it was enough to make any woman uncomfortable. He didn't want to give her any reason to want to leave or walk out. Not that she'd get very far after the sedative he'd mixed in with her drink took effect. But if any of the neighbors saw a woman wandering around, dazed and confused, it would put an end to the evening, and his life would be forfeit. No, it was best that he act the gentleman and keep his depraved thoughts under control.

"I hope it's not too strong for you," Westley chimed, sitting beside her on the sofa, but leaving enough space between them that his date could feel at ease.

"It's perfect, thank you," she replied. She lowered her hand, holding her cup just over her lap as the fingers of her opposite hand nervously tapped the side of the mug.

Quiet seconds ticked by until the uncomfortable silence was broken by the humming of Westley's vibrating phone. He pulled it from his pocket and glanced at the screen, his expression one of annoyance.

"I'm sorry, I have to take this," he said, regrettably, even with the risk of increasing the ire of his demanding, impatient king. He stood from his seat and stepped only a few feet from the sofa before clicking the button on his phone.

"Hi, Mom, this isn't the best time," he began. He brought his hand to his forehead and rubbed the frustration away as he listened. "Can't Charley take care of that for you? I know, Mom, but..." His words ended abruptly, interrupted by his mother's pleas. "All right. Fine. But I won't be able to get there until morning. Okay. No, it's not a problem. I love you, too. Bye."

He hung up and huffed, turning his attention first to the royal presence beside him, who bore his clenched teeth in aggravation, then to Gabby, a much softer sight on the eyes.

"I'm sorry about that," he offered. "My mother is getting to that age where things are becoming a bit difficult for her."

"I think it's sweet that you help your mother."

"Yeah, well, my brother is a lot closer, but he can't be bothered to do anything if it isn't for himself."

"Well, I'm sure your mother appreciates all that you do for her," Gabby said, smiling.

Westley reclaimed his spot on the sofa beside his date as she took another sip of her tainted coffee.

"Speaking of mothers," Westley began, "did I read on your online profile that your mother was a Broadway singer?"

"Yes," Gabby's face lit up. "My mother was incredible. She could sing, she could dance. She did it all. And beautiful, too."

"I bet! I mean, if her daughter is any indication of her beauty..."

Gabby waved her finger in front of her face with a smirk. "Actually, everyone tells me I look more like my Dad. I think I got all of his genes except for the scraggly mop on my head."

"Oh, come on," Westley said. "You have beautiful hair."

"The curls can be a bit much at times," Gabby added.

"I love the curls."

"Thank you."

Just then, Westley dipped his shoulder and screamed in pain, almost causing Gabby to spill her drink as she jolted sideways.

"What is it?" she questioned, panic in her voice.

He couldn't tell her about the invisible hand that had squeezed his shoulder in an iron grip. With the amount of pain he was feeling, he wasn't sure if he could get the words out to tell her anything at all. With his teeth clasped together tighter than a bear trap, and his face giving away his anguish, Westley swung his opposite fist up and smashed it into his ailing shoulder. He felt immediate relief as the harsh emperor released his hold, but the message had already been delivered, loud and clear. The unyielding monarch's patience had worn thin. A sacrifice had been demanded, the ransom due. He would wait no longer for the blood to spill from the flesh of these mortal shells.

The hardened ruler's eyes sparked with brilliance. Energy crackled between them as he drew his trusty sword from its sheath. Growling like a ferocious wolverine with spit expelling from his mouth, he swung the sword high overhead. Westley jumped from his seat and turned to face his would-be executioner.

"Wait!" he yelled.

At his sheep's sharp howl, the royal figure held fast, delaying his kill. Westley's eyes shifted sideways, peripherally noticing the horror in Gabby's face. He realized his sudden outburst would be scrutinized if he didn't quickly explain it away. He swiveled his upper body to face her.

"Sorry. That was loud. I meant, uh, can you wait here for a moment? I'll be right back. I have a problem I have to deal with." He took one step, then paused before adding, "The old shoulder injury, I mean. It sneaks up on me at the worst moments."

He stomped off and ducked into a bedroom doorway off the living room, staring heatedly at the large behemoth bearing down on him. He closed the door behind them and backed away from the already enraged king.

"What are you doing?" Westley questioned in an exasperated whisper. "We had a deal. I had until midnight to get you my replacement."

The bulky sovereign spoke through silent lips, words only Westley could hear.

"We're almost there," Westley argued, keeping his voice down. "She's been drinking the coffee. She'll be out in no time."

Again, words clamored in his ear from the one who lay claim to his life should the high price not be paid in time.

"You need to curb your royal temper, your majesty. You wanted to have your fun, to watch your victim suffer. You have to let this play out my way. You'll get your wish. You'll get your precious sacrifice. But a deal's a deal. I still have two hours. Now put the sword away."

The angry emperor growled.

"Please," Westley added.

Fiery eyes dimmed as the frustrated king breathed in, filling his lungs with nature's calming brew. He curled his upper lip to convey his dissatisfaction with having to wait longer, but as his unwilling pet reminded him, a deal was a deal. He would forego his urge for an early killing. He slid the sword back into its protective scabbard, snarling at Westley as he did.

"Okay," Westley whispered in relief. "Now, can we get back out there before she thinks I'm some kind of crazy lunatic?"

The annoyed king stepped aside to allow Westley access to the door. As they exited, Westley's heart pounded in his chest, and a grin fell upon his lips. The time was at hand. While they argued over the fate of a life soon forfeit, Gabby had fallen victim to the effects of the tranquilizer. Her body lay slanted over the arm of the sofa, her skirt wet and stained from the undrunk coffee that spilled from her overturned cup. Westley gazed up at the unruly presence by his side and let out an unsavory giggle.

"Let's have some fun."

Chapter 7

The first few drops of liquid on Gabby's slumped head did nothing. The next few awakened her from her daze as her eyes fluttered open, fighting with the heavy weight of her eyelids. Westley stood before her, holding a small glass of water. A blurred image was all she saw as she attempted to speak.

"Wh-where am I?" she stuttered, her voice barely audible. On her second effort, her words were almost a whisper. "What time...what time is it?"

"Time for you to be quiet," Westley said harshly.

At the sound of duct tape peeling free from its roll, Gabby's eyes flew open. She remembered it all. Her blind date with Westley. She was at his house. But what was going on? As Westley leaned forward to place the strip of tape over her mouth, her panicked reaction was to slap his hand away, but her arms didn't move. Instead, she felt the muscles in her shoulders strain, just then realizing her arms were bound behind her back.

She was sitting in a wooden chair in the center of Westley's living room, her wrists immobilized behind the backrest. She felt the adhesive of the duct tape pulling at her skin as she squirmed and tugged at her arms. She tried to kick instinctively, but they, too, were restrained, bound tightly to the legs of the chair. She screamed futilely, the sound coming through as merely a hushed mumble behind the silver strip covering her mouth. Her head began to shiver, and her eyes grew wide as she watched the expression on Westley's face change to that of satisfaction and pleasure.

She frantically mumbled more behind the tape, struggling to free herself, but to no avail. Westley flashed her a contented grin, pleased at his handiwork. He backed up into the kitchen and grabbed a second chair from the dining table, then placed it two feet in front of his lovely but unfortunate date. As he sat down to face her, he glanced up to his right at his towering liege and smiled.

"I told you I would do it," he said.

Gabby shifted her frightened eyes upward to her left to where Westley was focused, but she saw nothing but the ceiling. Westley turned his head to face his defenseless guest and let out a heavy sigh.

"I suppose you're wondering what this is all about," he said. "You probably think I'm crazy, that I'm a bad person. I'm neither of those things. I'm just an ordinary guy who found himself in an extraordinary predicament. You see, things weren't going to end well for me tonight had I not gotten you here. I suppose I could have resorted to drastic measures and tried to kidnap some unsuspecting person, but I've never done this before. They probably would have been uncooperative, as I'm sure kidnap victims often are. They make lots of noise, drawing unwanted attention to themselves. I couldn't have that. I'm on a strict deadline, and any delay would have surely cost me more than you know."

Suddenly, Westley's attention was averted to his right, as his face soured.

"Hey!" he yelled into the air beside himself. "I've got a little time here. If I'm going to do all the nasty things you want me to do, at least allow me the decency to explain why."

Gabby frantically darted her eyes around, looking for whoever it was Westley was talking to. Westley noticed her reaction and let out a half-chuckle.

"Oh, you must be wondering who I'm talking to. Silly me, you haven't been formally introduced. Allow me to present to you, in all his glory, my liege, my king, His Royal Majesty himself: the Emperor. That's right, I said the Emperor. Or, as *I* like to call him, a royal pain in my ass."

Westley flinched sideways and threw his hands up in front of his chest. "Hey, hey! Take it easy, big guy. It was just a joke. Shit! You really like pulling that thing out, don't you?"

Westley peered back at his bound date, her eyes like saucers.

"Oh, that wasn't anything sexual," he explained. "He's got a long sword he likes to play with." Westley scrunched his face, realizing his word choice didn't help matters. "What I mean is, he has an *actual* sword that he keeps threatening me with. Sorry, this is all new to me."

Gabby mumbled angrily behind the tape, jerking her head back and forth, fighting with the tape holding her arms. Or, perhaps, it was an attempt to headbutt her captor. Neither was successful.

"Listen," Westley continued, watching his date struggle, and perhaps, feeling a touch of guilt, "I know you're confused about all of this. It doesn't make much sense. *I* even have a hard time believing this to be real. But it is. It's all *too* real. I wish it weren't. I wish I could let you go, and we could continue where we left off on our date. But I can't do that. You see, I don't want to die tonight. But a ransom is due, and unless I trade a life for a life, that's exactly what's going to happen. *Your* death will save my life. You should be proud of that."

Gabby yelled into the tape, but only the sound of "Mmmm. Mmm mmm mmmm, mm mm mmm," came through.

"What was that?" Westley asked. "You want to know how all of this came to be?"

He took in a deep breath and exhaled. He pulled his phone out and looked at the time, then flashed it sideways to show his wraithlike ruler.

"Fifty-two minutes. What do you think, Your Majesty? Can I tell her before we get to the torture?"

The white-bearded sovereign snarled his disapproval, a growl for only Westley's ears to hear. The king's lips spoke their silent command, to which Westley replied, "Okay, I'll make it quick, then."

He looked at Gabby and rolled his eyes. "You'll have to forgive him; he's a bit impatient. But you need to understand, he comes from a different time, a different era. All of this is strange to him, just as his presence is strange to you and me. Well, except you can't see him, so my talking to the air is probably more strange to you. Anyway, I never meant for any of this to happen. To understand why I need to do this, why your sacrifice, though quite unfortunate, is a necessary evil, I'll have to take you back to ten days ago, back to when this burden fell upon my shoulders.

"I'd tell you to sit back and relax, but, well, you know. Even so, I think you should prepare yourself; this is going to be one hell of a wild ride."

Chapter 8

Westley scoffed at the sign above the fairground tent. "Tarot Reading" wasn't something he believed in, even if his niece did. She'd convinced him to take her when her father refused, stating he didn't want his daughter mixed up in, as he called it, "that spiritual mumbo-jumbo." Had Westley had a daughter of his own, he would have had a similar objection. But, since he and his brother, Charley, seemed to relish in each other's misery, Westley took the opportunity to infringe upon his older sibling's wishes.

"Thanks for bringing me, Uncle Wes," the teenager spouted, leading him toward the tent's split-canvas entrance.

"Anything to make your father upset with me, Darrow, you know that."

"I don't understand why you and Dad can't get along," Darrow said. "Grandma always tells me how you two were so close when you were younger."

"She says that, huh?"

Darrow nodded.

"Well, your Grandma is old and senile."

"Oh, my God! Stop that, Uncle Wes." She playfully slapped her uncle's upper arm.

"Okay," Westley jokingly flinched, side-stepping from his niece and putting his hands up defensively. "Mercy."

Darrow rolled her eyes.

"Let's just say that your Grandma isn't quite remembering things accurately," Westley continued. "Your father used to wrestle me to the ground and make me tap out of whatever holds he felt like putting me in on any given day. When I would cry out in pain, Grandma used to shush me, telling me I was being too loud. She always favored your father over me."

"Dad told me she always favored *you*," Darrow said, stopping outside the tent to finish their discussion before entering.

"That sounds like something he'd say."

Darrow tilted her head and gave her uncle an argumentative grin.

"Listen," Westley said, pointing up at the sign above the tent's entrance flaps, "are you doing this, or not?"

"Yeah, I am," she said excitedly, pushing aside one half of the canvas doorway and entering the dimmed space. Westley followed behind, shaking his head skeptically.

Within the tent, soft harp music emanated from small speakers hung at two opposing corners. A small card table sat on the dirt floor under the tent's peak with a lit antique oil lamp sitting upon it. Two folding chairs occupied the space, one at each end of the table. There was nobody else present.

Westley glanced around, curious about what they were supposed to do.

"So, ah, how does this work?" he asked his niece. "Do you sit? Is there a bell to ring for service?"

"I don't know," she replied. "I've never had a professional reading before."

"I hate to tell you this, Darrow," Westley spoke out of the side of his mouth, "but we're at a fairground. I'm not sure this qualifies as 'professional.'"

Suddenly, a woman's thick-accented voice erupted from outside the rear of the tent.

"You doubt the authenticity of Madam Vashon, naysayer?"

Westley's face paled with embarrassment as a flap in the rear tent wall burst open, exposing the eerie voice's owner. The woman, in her mid-sixties, wore a full-length, orange and purple dress, complete with a colorful, silk turban on her head. Heavily applied blue eye shadow splashed across her eyelids, while a thin, penciled black outline bordered her red lips. She had a tattoo of a black quarter-moon on her right cheek and a yellow sun on her left. She peered at her visitors in disapproval. Westley felt himself gulp.

"You have come for a reading, yes?" the woman asked without a smile.

"My niece…"

"I was not talking to you," the woman interrupted, her eyes focused on the teenage girl.

"Y-yes," Darrow answered, nodding.

With a grimace, the woman began glancing around the tent curiously as if she were hearing voices. Then, her eyes darted to Westley.

"Do you feel it?" she asked. "A darkness has entered. It is strong."

"N-no," he answered cautiously, subtly shaking his head.

"Perhaps it is *you* who should receive Madam Vashon's reading."

"Oh, no. That's fine," Westley said, putting a hand up to refuse. "This really isn't my thing."

"I see," the woman said, squinting.

After a few seconds of silence, during which the tarot reader kept her eyes locked on Westley's, she took in a deep breath and shifted a milder stare toward the girl.

"Please, sit down," the woman requested, gesturing to the empty chair near Darrow.

Darrow hesitated, glancing at her uncle first before deciding to heed the woman's words. The woman, dressed in extravagant Middle Eastern garb, took her place across from Darrow. Westley stepped behind his niece's chair and observed over her shoulder as the woman placed her palms, side by side, faced down on the table. A moment later, she lifted them to reveal a stack of faded cards.

"That was neat," Westley unintentionally murmured under his breath.

The tarot reader shifted her eyes up, giving Westley an annoyed stare. She divided the cards into five piles, strategically placing them into the shape of a plus sign, followed by a column of four to the right of it. Darrow watched sharply in anticipation.

Before continuing, the woman looked at Darrow and asked, "What is it you seek?"

Darrow stuttered, "I, um, I-I, I don't..."

"Enlightenment, obviously," Westley jumped in snarkily to aid his struggling niece.

"Remain silent!" the woman barked, raising her voice sternly.

"Sorry," Westley replied after he'd jumped a bit.

"Now, I ask again," the woman spoke in a much kinder tone, peering back at her querent, "what is it you seek?"

"I guess, I don't know," Darrow began nervously, "I just thought it would be cool to learn if I'm heading on the right track. Like, if my future looks promising."

"I see," the woman responded.

Westley rolled his eyes, which didn't go unnoticed by the reader. She looked down at the cards and mumbled something quietly in her native tongue, or perhaps, as Westley decided, in a made-up language, before stating louder, "Let's begin."

She reached for the center card and flipped it over, revealing The Moon.

"The Moon signifies anxiety and fear," the woman began. "You are nervous about what is to come. But don't be alarmed. The world around you is but an illusion, waiting to be shaped by your will. Tread lightly, however, for each decision you make carries a price."

Darrow licked her dry lips and nodded, her eyes wide. The woman flipped the card to the left of center, revealing The Hanged Man. The flame in the oil lamp flickered. Westley and Darrow shifted their stare to the flame, while the Middle Eastern woman stared only at Westley.

"Think about all that you are," the woman continued, "and surrender only to what drives you. The Hanged Man is not a card to be feared, but embraced. Let it guide you down a stronger path so that you might learn from your experiences. Only if followed by The Devil card should The Hanged Man be of worry, for it is then that one's perspective can deceive them."

The reader then flipped the card farthest from Darrow, and the lamp's flame ignited brighter, causing Darrow to flinch. When she looked back at the cards, she gasped. The Devil stared her down.

The tarot reader huffed through her nose and smirked. "The Devil hides his true form in shadow and persuasion. Heed my words. The clearest path is sometimes the darkest. Do not be fooled by your own ignorance. If you do not fight the temptation and seek out an alternative, it will lure you into his clutches, which leads to only one outcome."

The woman glanced up at Westley before looking back into Darrow's worried eyes. "Do you understand?"

Darrow aggressively nodded her response. Westley felt irritation growing inside. He knew teenagers were highly impressionable and could be heavily influenced by what the woman was spewing. He could sense his niece's trepidation, her fears hanging on the woman's every word. But still, he let the woman continue her charade.

She flipped the card to the right of center. The flame in the oil lamp immediately dimmed and then extinguished. There was still enough daylight seeping in through the tent's front opening to see the Death card displayed. Westley saw his niece's shoulders tighten before him.

"Death is not always an end," the woman spoke. "It can mean a transition from an old life into a new. A transformation into something beautiful, like a butterfly emerging from its cocoon, shedding its ugly past for a brighter future."

Darrow's shoulders relaxed as she let out a breath in relief. The reader shifted her eyes to the girl's uncle.

"Or it can just mean death," the woman added.

Westley had heard enough. "Oh, come on!" he erupted. "Are you trying to scare her? Do you get off on that sort of thing?"

The woman remained calm, looking at Westley through cold, disciplined eyes. "Madam Vashon only reads the cards as they lie."

"As *they* lie?" Westley questioned heatedly. "Or as *you* lie?"

"Madam Vashon speaks only the truth," the woman replied through clenched teeth. "The cards are dealt for the fate of the individual seeking answers. Remember, *you* came to *me*."

"Well, now we're leaving," Westley protested. "Come on, Darrow."

Darrow stayed seated, staring at the cards in front of her. "No. I-I want her to finish."

"But honey, this isn't real. It doesn't mean anything."

Madam Vashon curled her upper lip at his comment.

"I want her to finish, Uncle Wes."

Westley huffed as his shoulders dropped.

"But Darrow..."

"I want her to finish."

Westley pursed his lips and relented. "Fine. She can finish up this little cross here," he pointed to the cards in the center, "and then we're going."

The woman looked across at Darrow for her acceptance to continue. Darrow swallowed hard and nodded.

The reader reached across to the card closest to her querent and flipped it over. The wick in the oil lamp ignited with a flame that leapt over the top of the glass before dwindling to normal size.

"Nice theatrics," Westley blurted, still annoyed.

The woman sneered at his remark.

"The curse has been set. The last card is revealed. Darkness will come to deliver the bearer unto the hands of death. The Moon, The Hanged Man, The Devil, Death, and this, the final card, cannot be ignored. The fates have spoken. Only a bounty paid in blood can reverse what is to come next. Decide carefully the life from whom the blood is spilled."

"This is horseshit," Westley stated angrily. "I can't believe they let you tell these things to people. Especially to kids."

The woman peered at Westley through narrowed eyes. "The reading was not your niece's; it was yours."

Westley's eyes opened wide as he curled his upper lip in disgust. "Darrow, no more arguing. We're leaving. Let's go."

His niece stood from her chair and stepped past him as he pulled open the front flap of the tent to let her exit. Before he could step out, the tarot reader exclaimed in her heavy accent, "Ten days!"

Westley stopped and turned in curiosity. "What?"

"A visitor will come," she replied. "He will ask for his ransom in blood. You must decide. Is there a life worth less who can save you from the fate you have been dealt?" She motioned to the cards on the table. "You have ten days. Choose wisely whose existence you condemn."

Westley shook his head. "Whatever."

As he walked out of the tent, the woman looked down at the arrangement, the final card drawn. The Emperor, with all his authority, always demanded a heavy toll.

Chapter 9

Westley peered at his quivering date. A bead of sweat dripped from Gabby's forehead down the bridge of her nose, where it trickled sideways into the corner of her left eye. The stinging sensation caused her to squeeze her eyes shut and voice her discomfort into the duct tape's adhesive.

"And wouldn't you know it," Westley stated over her grumbles, continuing his story. "That goddamn tarot reader lady was right. I received a visitor the very next night. This grand piece of royalty that stands beside me." He swung both arms to his right as if he were a game show assistant showcasing a prize. "I'll admit, he scared the shit out of me when he first showed up in my bedroom. I almost wet the bed when I awoke to the sight. I know that sounds gross, but if you could see him, you'd understand why."

Then, Westley yelled out. "Ow!" He snapped his arms back to his chest and vigorously rubbed his right hand.

"It's called a joke, man. Don't they have a sense of humor back where you come from? Christ."

He turned to face his bound hostage.

"He's a little touchy," Westley said, nodding his head sideways. Then he leaned in and whispered, "He slapped my hand like a little bitch."

Gabby mumbled incoherently.

"What was that?" Westley asked, putting his hand up behind his ear.

She mumbled again.

"I didn't catch that. One more time."

Again, only gibberish behind the tape.

"Here, let me help," he said.

Westley peeled away a corner of the tape enough to let Gabby speak.

"You're crazy!" she said, her lips quavering.

"I'm really not," Westley responded.

"Then let me go."

"I can't do that."

"I won't tell anyone."

"You don't get it, do you? That woman, 'Madam Vashon,' she was telling the truth. She cursed me with those cards, or her voodoo magic, or something. I wouldn't be surprised if my brother somehow put her up to it. I wasn't even the one seeking the reading. But I digress, back to the real issue. The king here, he told me, I'd soon be dead if I didn't find another to replace me. Hell, it's taken everything I've had to keep him from killing me early. But the rules are the rules. I was given ten days. In case you haven't figured it out yet," Westley snickered, "that's today."

"Why me?" Gabby questioned.

"It's nothing personal," Westley offered, as if that would make his captive feel better. "In fact, I went back to the fairgrounds to see the tarot reader. I was going to kill *her* for doing this to me. The tent was dark. Nobody would've seen a thing. I could have crept in and out without a soul knowing I was even there."

"Why didn't you do it, then?" Gabby asked. "Kill her, I mean."

Westley shook his head in regret. "It's like something out of a B-grade horror movie, or maybe from a book by that crappy author, Jeff VanOudenhove."

Gabby cringed. "Eewww, that *is* bad. He's the worst."

"I know, right? Anyway," Westley contin-ued, "the goddamn place was shut down. Eve-rything had been packed up. It was just an empty field. I was like, fuck! What am I going to do? I didn't want to have to kill someone I knew. Then it dawned on me. What if I set up an online dating profile? I just needed a body - someone to bring back to my house. I'll tell ya, I'd almost given up. I couldn't get a match to save my life. Oops, no pun intended. But then, like a miracle, *you* came along. Thank you for that."

Gabby shook her head and sneered. "Don't expect a 'You're welcome,' you sick, son of a bitch."

"Don't worry, I'm not." Westley looked at his phone and crinkled his nose. "Well, we've only got twenty-three minutes until midnight. I'm afraid we're going to have to get this show on the road. I wanted to make it quick, but the big guy here wants me to take my time tortur-ing you."

Gabby shook her head. "You don't have to do that."

"Oh, but I do; I kinda promised him."

Westley got up, walked to the kitchen, and grabbed the steak knife from the counter. Gabby's eyes widened as she furiously began to struggle with her bonds. Her captor took his seat and smiled at her tenderly, raising the knife in front of her face. "Where should we begin?"

Just then, a knocking sounded at the side door. Before Gabby could scream, Westley slapped the tape back over her mouth.

"You shut up!" Westley said quietly through gritted teeth. "Do you hear me? Make a sound, and I'll kill whoever it is at the door. Their death will be on your hands. Then I'll come back and kill you anyway. Got it?"

Gabby nodded her head.

Westley stood and looked at the Emperor. "Don't worry, I'll get rid of whoever it is. You keep watch over her." He slid the knife into his back pocket and stormed through the kitchen toward the side door. He lifted the shade to see that it was his neighbor, Alex. He opened the door a few inches and leaned his head out.

"Hey, Alex. What's going on? It's really late."

Alex stared at Westley with glossy eyes, a confused look on his face, jiggling keys in his hand.

With his words slurred, Alex answered, "What the hell are you doing in my house?" His body wobbled a bit as he tried to maintain his balance. "You already changed the god-damn locks on me? Does my wife know? Wait, are you fucking her?"

Westley glared impatiently at his inebriated neighbor. "Alex, you're drunk. This is *my* house." He pointed across the driveway at the next house over. "That's your house over there."

Alex turned to see where Westley was pointing, almost falling over. He scratched his head in confusion. "That place looks shitty," Alex stated. "Are you sure I can't stay here with you?"

"No, Alex. Go home. Get some sleep."

"Party pooper," Alex said while he struggled to descend the two steps leading to level ground. "Thanks for the lift home, man," he continued, waving over his shoulder as he wobbled across to his own yard.

Westley shook his head and closed the door. He pulled the knife from his back pocket and stepped into the living room's entryway, an annoyed look on his face.

"Now, where were we?"

Chapter 10

Gabby shook her head emphatically as Westley stepped closer, flashing the knife threateningly. The smile on his face grew, anticipating what was coming as if he were going to enjoy it. Gabby's eyes widened with fear. She began screaming into the tape covering her mouth, the sounds coming out as struggling mumbles, trying to burst free. She yanked her arms with all her might and tried thrashing her legs to no avail. She was helpless.

"Will you stop squirming?" Westley demanded. "It will all be over soon. There isn't much time left, so I'm only going to cut you a few times to please His Lordship over here." Westley nodded his head to the side to acknowledge the elder being that Gabby couldn't see. "Then, I'm afraid, I'll have to end your life. Trust me; this works out better for you. If the Emperor had his way, the torture would have lasted for hours. But time is of the essence, a luxury I don't have."

Westley leaned in, bringing the knife to within inches of Gabby's left cheek.

"Here we go," he said, with as much antic-ipated excitement as a child opening a present.

Gabby turned her head to her right and tightened her jaw as the blade touched her skin. That's when she noticed the coffee table, or rather, what was *on* the coffee table. Her heart pounded as exhilaration washed over her. She bobbed her head back and forth like a chicken while shouting something deliberate and repeatedly behind the duct tape. Westley noticed her odd behavior and pulled the knife back. Gabby had her eyes trained on the far end of the sofa where she had earlier sat. Westley glanced over curiously, then back to his captive.

"What?" he questioned.

Gabby flashed her eyes insistently toward the sofa. "Mm mmmm!" She cried. "Mm mmmm!"

Westley huffed, rolling his eyes.

"Hold on," he said. He pulled at one corner of the tape, peeling it back until it hung from Gabby's opposite cheek. "What is it?"

"My purse," she said, catching her breath while nodding her chin to the arm of the sofa.

Westley looked again and noticed the leather strap slung over the armrest, blending in with the sofa.

"What about it?" he asked.

"You need to see something," she replied.

"What do I need to see?" Westley questioned.

"Go and look in the front pocket."

"Is this a joke?" he asked, furrowing his brow.

"Just go!" Gabby repeated excitedly.

Westley tilted his head, staring her down, wondering what could be so important in her purse as to divert her attention from imminent danger. His curiosity intensified. He turned his head to the clock on the wall. He had twelve minutes remaining. He reasoned he still had plenty of time to kill her if she were simply trying to delay the inevitable. He could jab the knife into her throat and end it all in an instant. He backed away, pointing the knife in her direction.

"If you're playing with me, I swear to God I'm going to cut your eyes out." He glanced over at the ancient ruler and winked. "You'd like that, wouldn't you?"

The Emperor snarled silent words.

"I'm going!" Westley expressed eagerly. "Relax already!"

He walked over and plucked Gabby's purse from the floor beside the sofa. He unzipped the center pouch and spread it apart.

"Not there," Gabby called out. "The front pocket."

"I'd better not find a badge in here." He undid the metal snap holding the front pocket closed and looked inside. His nose crinkled in confusion. He reached in and pulled out a little glass medicine bottle. Squeezing it between his thumb and index finger, he read the label, sounding out the syllables. "Chlora-fentra-atra-peen. What the hell is this?"

Gabby's shoulders dropped as she let out a relieved breath. "You sure took your sweet time."

Westley looked over at her. "What was that?"

Gabby shifted her eyes in his direction and smiled. "I wasn't talking to you."

Just then, Westley's eyelids exploded open as his king's body jerked forward in agony. "What the fu…" His words were cut short as he watched a gaping hole burst in the Emperor's chest. Blood spewed first from the open wound, and then from the large figure's mouth, turning his once white beard a vibrant red. A moment later, the sovereign leader fell to his knees, gasping and clutching his chest in disbelief, before crumpling face-first to the floor.

"Wh-what the hell just happened?" Westley questioned, frozen with dread.

"He's dead, isn't he?" Gabby asked, smirking.

"You!" Westley yelled. "You did that to him?"

She slowly shook her head. "Not me."

"Then who?"

Westley watched as Gabby turned her head and looked at the empty air over the king's dead body. Then she swiveled it back to him.

"I think you should stop talking now."

Westley felt his heart beating against his ribs as anger gripped him. He couldn't believe the helpless woman would speak to him so brazenly. He tried to take a step, but his leg wouldn't respond to his command. His hand holding the little glass bottle began to tremble. A moment later, he lost all feeling in his fingers. The bottle slipped from his grip, hitting the floor, and rolled on its side until it came to rest at Gabby's right foot.

"What's happening?" Westley questioned, his voice filled with fear. "Why can't I feel my arms?"

Gabby glanced over her shoulder with eagerness. "Would you mind helping me out?" A second later, the sound of duct tape ripping rang out. Gabby's arms sprang forward.

"Finally!" she said, with the strip of duct tape still clinging to her cheek. She clawed at the remaining tape around her wrists while the tape at her ankles suddenly split and tore free.

Westley stood frozen, his body beginning to wobble as his legs weakened. Gabby stood from the chair and pointed to the coffee table.

"I see you drank your coffee," she said nonchalantly.

Without thinking, Westley answered, "While you were unconsc...wait! You drugged my coffee?"

"You drugged mine first, you ass."

"Well, yeah, but that's different. I had no choice."

Gabby shook her head and turned her eyes away from him.

"You can put the sword away now," she said. "I can handle things from here."

"Wh-who are you talking to?" Westley questioned, his voice becoming quieter as his vocal cords numbed.

"Oh, I'm sorry," Gabby responded. "How rude of me. I thought you'd have figured it out by now. I didn't realize you were that dumb. As you said, that Madam Vashon bitch; she sure knows her tarot cards."

Westley looked at her, puzzled.

"That's right," she continued. "I visited her, too. It must have been earlier that same day." Gabby let out a chuckle. "What are the odds the cards would fall as they had? Twice. The Moon, The Hanged Man, The Devil, Death, and in your case, The Emperor. But in mine," she glanced behind her, "it was the Empress."

Westley felt his knees give way, and he teetered sideways, falling onto the couch, immobile.

"Ten days," Gabby continued. "I thought I was a goner for sure. But then some idiot agreed to a date. All I had to do was get him someplace where we could be alone. Maybe I could get him to take me to his place. Well, that was easier than I thought it would be. Can I let you in on a little secret? That guy in the hotel lobby – I have no idea who he was; I'd never seen him before."

She pulled the remaining piece of tape from her cheek.

"I have to admit," Gabby continued, "I'm a little disappointed at how slow-acting the paralytic took effect. Honestly, I was a little worried I wouldn't get the opportunity to pour it into your drink at all. But when you suddenly walked off into the bedroom..." She rolled her eyes. "Well, I now understand why. These Royal Highnesses can be real pricks, can't they?"

She glanced at the clock. "Anyway, we're kind of out of time. I've only got three minutes to get this done."

She stepped forward and pulled the knife free from Westley's loose hand, smiling at him. "As you so eloquently put it, it's nothing personal. I just don't want to die tonight. So, while you were busy playing checkers, I was playing chess. And everyone knows that in chess," her eyes shifted to the Empress, "the Queen is the most powerful piece."

Gabby smiled devilishly as she gripped the knife in a tight fist, ready to trade a life for a life. After all, it was the heavy ransom due. Westley wouldn't scream. He wouldn't make a noise. She made sure of that. Like the rest of him, his vocal cords were paralyzed. As for herself, she was ready to be free of her curse.

With a triumphant grin on her face, and with only two minutes to spare, the blade of the knife drew blood.

Read on for a sneak peek of the horror suspense novel
Reaper House

Available on Amazon

Prologue

The house lay dormant for nearly two decades. Its dreary, silent walls remained lifeless and empty after the incident, telling no further tales of the horror that took place beyond the doors on that fateful night, other than the grueling images captured by the crime scene investigators' cameras. What was once a place for devilishly fun, frightful scares during the witching season soon became a house of horrors none would ever forget. On that cold October evening, when monsters lurked around every corner, begging for their treats, another kind of monster was stirring deep in the recesses of Isabelle Unger's soul.

Neither the history books nor the newspaper articles written about the horrific tragedy could tell you what caused Isabelle to snap on that Halloween night in 2009, only that she killed twelve people behind the locked doors of Reaper House.

For thirty-nine years, Reaper House, located on the outskirts of Templeton, Massachusetts, was a favorite attraction for thrill-seekers of everything ghoulish and ghastly during the month of October.

Opened in 1970 by George and Isabelle Unger to a small, local reception of thirteen fervent individuals, a number the married couple considered lucky, the lavish yet eerie haunted house was available for public viewing for only five nights. Though the props were rudimentary and the scares ascetic, with an array of human-like animatronics fashioned to look like butchers and psychotic torturers in a grand production to entertain teenage and adult horror enthusiasts alike, Reaper House became a cherished, unique experience for all visitors. For five years, the Ungers continued tours on the same five-day schedule, opening on October 27th and closing promptly on October 31st at 11:59 pm. The house's popularity soon grew from word of mouth until people traveled from across the state and beyond to enter the haunted halls of the enormous mansion. Beginning in 1976, because of the steady increase in visitors, George and Isabelle decided to increase the number of days Reaper House was open to the public to nine days leading up to Halloween.

The 8,030 square-foot mansion played the largest role, looking like it had been built on a backlot of a large movie studio, ominously overlooking the dirt road from its perch atop a secluded hill, much like Norman Bates' house in the movie Psycho that scared audiences ten years earlier. Each year, the Ungers would add props and animatronics more terrifying than the year before, enthralling newcomers and increasing returning visitors' anticipation.

Throughout Reaper House's history, the Ungers, a known superstitious couple, held onto the belief that thirteen was a lucky number since that was the number of customers they had on their first night. For that reason, only thirteen individuals were allowed entrance into the house at any one time. Only after all thirteen people had exited the premises through the back, where they would weave their way along a path through a spooky cemetery, would the next thirteen be allowed to enter through the front. The tours would take place in twenty-minute intervals, with George and Isabelle rotating shifts during the house's daily operating hours.

By 1992, the haunted house had increased its daily operations to thirteen nights leading up to Halloween. The steady increase in price each year, as well as the growing number of visitors, made it possible for the Ungers to update the mansion further, adding secret passages and hidden rooms to the already exciting tours. But, in 2003, George Unger, at the age of fifty-five, died of respiratory failure due to complications from pneumonia, leaving his widowed Isabelle alone with the burden of maintaining Reaper House.

For six years, Isabelle continued with her and her husband's legacy, though it became harder to keep up with the scheduled tours since she was now alone and growing long in years.

Nobody could know the stresses Isabelle endured after the passing of her husband or what thoughts haunted her dreams each night. But on October 31st, 2009, on a dark and dreary Halloween night, eight teenagers and five adults entered Reaper House for the last time. The doors locked behind them, as they always had, and no more visitors entered after them.

After multiple complaints from waiting parents and customers, which drew the authorities to the property, the doors to Reaper House were forced open, to the sheer horror of the responding officers. The bodies of twelve individuals were found in different rooms of the house in various conditions. Most had been cut or stabbed in one way or another. Two had died from suffocation, with plastic bags still wrapped around their heads. And at least one unlucky visitor had been dismembered, their limbs stacked like firewood in front of the fireplace. It was later reported that authorities believed one victim possibly escaped, since they didn't recover a thirteenth body from inside the house, though it was never confirmed, since the victim never came forward to tell their story.

Isabelle was found sitting in the dark in the mansion's study in a large wingback chair, rocking her upper body back and forth and laughing uncontrollably. She was holding a bloody knife in one hand and a small hatchet in the other, her clothes covered in blood. When the police entered the room where she sat, their flashlights shining on the woman's disturbing appearance, her laughter ceased, and she turned her maniacal stare in their direction.

"The Reaper comes for us all" was heard as an ominous whisper leaving the woman's pale lips before she turned the knife on herself, jamming it into the side of her neck.

Thirteen bodies in all were removed that day. Tainted walls and floors were scrubbed clean of the blood. But the memories of what happened in Reaper House reverberated long after the dead were buried. With no known relatives to claim the property, the mansion was eventually seized and abandoned by the town, left to wither and decay from the effects of time, the dirt access road gated and locked. Reaper House was no more.

Or was it?

A LETTER FROM THE AUTHOR

Dear readers,

I hope you loved *A King's Ransom*. I was fortunate enough to have been asked to participate in this multi-author collaboration series. I wasn't sure I would have time to commit to writing the story, as I had already begun my next novel, Zero Tolerance, but since it was only a short story between 10k and 15k words, I jumped right in anyway.

If you enjoyed the story, I'd be very grateful if you'd consider writing a review. I love to hear what readers think, which helps me grow as an author, and it makes such a difference in helping new readers discover my books for the first time.

Check out my website at:

javo-publication.square.site

Where signed copies of all of my books can be purchased. You can also find them on Amazon or ask your local bookstore to order them.

Thank you so much for your kind support!
Jeff

Enjoy these other great titles!

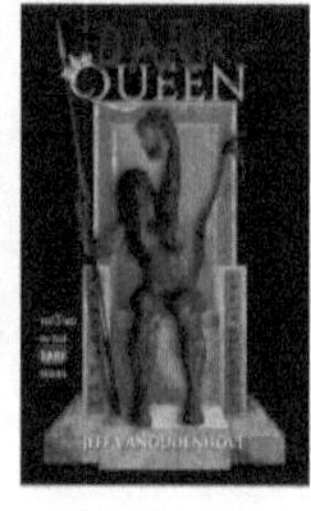

Acknowledgments

I would like to first thank my editor, Elizabeth Kelly, who, once again, offered her services to better this story. She has been by my side from my very first novel and yet somehow continues to put up with me.

Thank you, Erica Damon, for thinking of me and inviting me to be a part of this incredible series. It was fun.

Thank you, Maria Ann Green, for the fantastic cover. It turned out better than I could have hoped.

Thank you to all the wonderful authors who collaborated on making this series something special for readers to collect and enjoy.

And finally, to all my friends and family who have supported and encouraged me to continue writing, thank you. I couldn't have done it without you.

On to the next.

Jeff VanOudenhove has written several novels in the genre of dark fiction, including the **Dark Series** (supernatural suspense), **The Alphabet Killer Series** (crime thriller), **Just Listen** (psychological suspense thriller), **Emma** (YA psychological thriller), **Screams in the Dark and Other Twisted Tales** (short story collection), **Reaper House** (horror suspense), and **The Disappearing** (psychological thriller). His talent for storytelling combines unforgettable characters and dire situations, mixed with astonishing plot twists. **A King's Ransom** is Jeff's fourteenth book.